If you hold my hand

Written by Jillian Harker
Illustrated by Andy Everitt-Stewart

Oakey's mum opened the front door. "Come on, Oakey. Let's go outside and explore."

ROSE COTTAGE

But Oakey wasn't really sure. He was only small, and the world looked big and scary.

"Only if you promise to hold my hand," said Oakey.

So Oakey's mum led him down the long lane.
Oakey wished he was back at home again!

"This looks like a great place to play. Shall we take a look? What do you say?" asked Oakey's mum.

"Only if you hold my hand," said Oakey.

And Oakey did it!

"Look at me! I can do it!" he cried.

"This slide looks fun. Would you like to try?" asked Oakey's mum.

Oakey looked at the ladder. It stretched right up to the sky.

"I'm only small," said Oakey. "I don't know if I can climb that high — *unless you hold my hand.*"

And Oakey did it!

"Wheee! Did you see me?" he cried.

"We'll take a short cut through the wood," said Oakey's mum.

"I'm not sure if we should," said Oakey. "It looks dark in there. Well, I suppose we could—*will you hold my hand?*"

And Oakey did it!
"Boo! I scared you!" he cried.

Deep in the wood,
Oakey found a stream,
shaded by beautiful
tall trees.

And Oakey did it!

One...

two...

three...

four....

"Your turn now, Mum," cried Oakey,
holding out his hand.

Beyond the wood, Oakey and his mum
ran up the hill, and all the way
down to the sea.

"Come on, Oakey," called his mum.

"Would you like to paddle in the sea with me?"

But the sea looked **big**, and he was only small.

Suddenly, Oakey
knew that didn't
matter at all.
He turned to
his mum and

smiled...

"I can do **anything** if you hold my hand," he said.